Blackbeard the pirate was fierce and strong, with wild hair and a massive beard. He carried six pistols and a huge cutlass.

Blackbeard and his crew plundered the coast of Virginia in America.

by Barrie Wade and Graham Philpot

W
FRANKLIN WATTS
LONDON•SYDNEY

This is a story about Blackbeard, but he was a real person. It is thought that his name was Edward Teach and that he was born in Bristol, England. He became a pirate in around 1714, stealing ships around the shores of Jamaica and the east coast of America. He died in 1718.

First published in 2010 by
Franklin Watts
338 Euston Road
London NW1 3BH

Franklin Watts Australia
Level 17/207 Kent Street
Sydney NSW 2000

A CIP catalogue record for this book is available
from the British Library.

ISBN 978 0 7496 9437 1 (hbk)
ISBN 978 0 7496 9443 2 (pbk)

Series Editor: Jackie Hamley
Series Advisor: Catherine Glavina
Series Designer: Peter Scoulding

Printed in China

Franklin Watts is a division of
Hachette Children's Books,
an Hachette UK company
www.hachette.co.uk

His largest ship had 40 cannon, and could blast other ships right out of the water. Many sailors were too scared of him to leave harbour.

One day, Blackbeard held a wild party on Ocracoke Island, just down the coast.

When the Governor of Virginia
found out about the party, he
sent for Captain Maynard.

"You must get rid of Blackbeard," said the Governor. "He's been drinking rum on Ocracoke Island for two days and he only has a small ship there. This is your best chance."

9

"I'll need a small ship too," said
Maynard. "The water around that
island is too shallow for large ships
with cannon."

"Take swords and guns instead,"
said the Governor, "and two ships
to be safe."

So Maynard and his crew set off.
Soon they found Blackbeard's ship
in a shallow bay behind sandbanks.

The pirate party was in full swing.

13

"They must have seen us,"
said the helmsman.
"They think we can't sail into that
shallow water," Maynard replied,
"but our ships are light enough.
We'll attack them when the
water rises at high tide."

14

Blackbeard's men drank, shouted and sang all night. Nobody slept.

Next morning, Maynard's ships
floated in with the tide.
All was quiet.

Suddenly, a cannonball, fired from Blackbeard's ship, smashed into one of Maynard's ships.

"How did they get cannon in there?" cried the helmsman. "They've tricked us!"

"Yes," cried Maynard. "But that blast has blown them back onto a sandbank. They're stuck. Now, let us trick them."

Maynard ordered his men to hide.
Only he and the helmsman stayed
on deck as they raced towards
Blackbeard's ship.

The ships crashed. Wood splintered. Pirates staggered. Blackbeard lit the strings twisted into his hair.

"Board her, my lads, and tie up these two prisoners!" he roared.

But when the pirates jumped on board Maynard's ship, the other sailors rushed out of hiding.

"Ambush!" screamed Blackbeard,
his whole head smoking.

Cutlasses swung. Daggers flashed. Bullets flew. Blackbeard fought wildly...

...until a sword slash chopped his head clean off. He fell dead, and the other pirates gave in.

The seas around Virginia were safe again. But to this day, sailors tell stories of a headless ghost near Ocracoke Island...

29

Put these pictures in the correct order.
Which event do you think is most important?
Now try writing the story in your own words!

Puzzle 2

1. Come on, lads. Let's party!

2. Hide until he comes on board.

3. I will stop Blackbeard!

4. I order you to stop his pirating ways.

5. They'll never catch me here!

6. The seas will not be safe if you fail to stop him.

Choose the correct speech bubbles for the characters above. Can you think of any others? Turn over to find the answers.

Answers

Puzzle 1

The correct order is: 1f, 2b, 3c, 4e, 5d, 6a

Puzzle 2

Blackbeard: 1, 5

Captain Maynard: 2, 3

Governor of Virginia: 4, 6

Look out for more Hopscotch Adventures:

Aladdin and the Lamp
ISBN 978 0 7496 6692 7

Blackbeard the Pirate
ISBN 978 0 7496 6690 3

George and the Dragon
ISBN 978 0 7496 6691 0

Jack the Giant-Killer
ISBN 978 0 7496 6693 4

Beowulf and Grendel
ISBN 978 0 7496 8551 5*
ISBN 978 0 7496 8563 8

Agnes and the Giant
ISBN 978 0 7496 8552 2*
ISBN 978 0 7496 8564 5

The Dragon and the Pudding
ISBN 978 0 7496 8549 2*
ISBN 978 0 7496 8561 4

Finn MacCool and the Giant's Causeway
ISBN 978 0 7496 8550 8*
ISBN 978 0 7496 8562 1

Pirate Jack and the Inca Treasure
ISBN 978 0 7496 9438 8*
ISBN 978 0 7496 9444 9

Captain Kidd: Pirate Hunter
ISBN 978 0 7496 9439 5*
ISBN 978 0 7496 9445 6

Pirates of the Storm
ISBN 978 0 7496 9440 1*
ISBN 978 0 7496 9446 3

TALES OF SINBAD THE SAILOR

Sinbad and the Ogre
ISBN 978 0 7496 8559 1*
ISBN 978 0 7496 8571 3

Sinbad and the Whale
ISBN 978 0 7496 8553 9*
ISBN 978 0 7496 8565 2

Sinbad and the Diamond Valley
ISBN 978 0 7496 8554 6*
ISBN 978 0 7496 8566 9

Sinbad and the Monkeys
ISBN 978 0 7496 8560 7*
ISBN 978 0 7496 8572 0

For more Hopscotch Adventures and other Hopscotch books, visit:
www.franklinwatts.co.uk

* hardback